Perfectly Orange Princess Has a Ball

by Alyssa Crowne

illustrated by Charlotte Alder

Scholastic Inc.

New York   Toronto   London   Auckland
Sydney   Mexico City   New Delhi   Hong Kong

For Princess Hana and Princess Ava,
and their mother, Queen Ellie.

Thanks for your help and inspiration!

ISBN 978-0-545-20850-5

12 11 10 9 8 7 6 5 4 3   11 12 13 14 15/0

Printed in the U.S.A.   40

Designed by Kevin Callahan
First printing, August 2010

Contents

Chapter One

A Real Ball!

Kristina Kim climbed down the steps of the school bus. Grandma Soo was waiting by the front door of their house, just like she did every day.

Kristina raced down the walk. She waved a piece of orange paper in her hand.

"Grandma Soo! Grandma Soo, look!" she cried.

Peter, her younger brother, ran past her. He gave Grandma Soo a big hug. Then he turned and stuck his tongue out at Kristina.

"Ha! I beat you!" he said.

"Peter, be nice to your big sister," Grandma Soo said. "Now go inside and wash your hands. There is some fruit on the table if you're hungry."

Peter ran inside.

"Grandma Soo, there's going to be a real ball!" Kristina said. She held out the piece of paper. "Everyone in school is invited. We get to wear costumes. And there will be music and dancing and —"

"Slow down, Kristina," Grandma Soo said with a smile. "I see that you are excited, but it is chilly out here. Come inside and tell me more."

Kristina *was* very excited. But she

followed her grandmother inside. She always listened to Grandma Soo! Kristina hung her orange backpack on a hook in the hallway. She put her sweater in the closet. Peter's backpack and jacket were on the floor.

On another day, Kristina would have told on Peter. But not today. She wanted to talk about the ball! She followed Grandma Soo into the kitchen.

"Read it, Grandma," Kristina said, handing her grandmother the orange sheet of paper. "It tells all about the ball."

Grandma Soo read the invitation.

"'A Fall Ball,'" Grandma Soo read. "That sounds like a nice party."

"It's not just a party, it's a *ball*!" Kristina corrected her. "Just like in a fairy tale, with dancing and everything. And I get to wear a costume! Can you guess what I'll be?"

Grandma Soo's dark eyes twinkled. "Let me think. You will be . . . a cowgirl?"

Kristina put her hands on her hips. "No, Grandma!"

"Hmm. A witch?" Grandma asked.

Kristina shook her head. "No!"

"Maybe you will be a ghost, then," Grandma Soo said.

"Grandma! You *know* what I'm going to dress up as," Kristina told her. "A princess!"

Grandma Soo smiled. "Ah, a princess. I didn't know you liked princesses."

Kristina realized her grandmother was teasing. She smiled back. "Of *course* I do! And I have to dress like a princess if I'm going to a fancy ball."

"You will need a princess dress," Grandma Soo said.

Kristina thought about that for a minute. "I can wear my dress from last Halloween," she said.

"It might not fit you," Grandma Soo said. "You have grown very tall since last year."

"Chloe and Melissa have both grown more than me," Kristina replied, thinking of her two best friends. "Maybe it will still fit."

"If it's too small, I might be able to fix it," Grandma Soo said. She was very good at sewing things.

Kristina jumped up from her chair. "I'll go get it!"

She ran up the stairs to her bedroom. Her little black kitten, Pixie, was fast asleep on her bed. The sun was shining through her orange curtains. It made everything in the room look orange.

Kristina loved her room! She had bright orange walls and a pretty orange bedspread. The color orange made her feel happy inside. Her father always said she had lots of energy, and that's why she liked orange so much.

The year before, Kristina had wanted to be a princess for Halloween. But none of the princess costumes in the Halloween store were orange! Her mom had found the perfect orange dress on sale at the regular store. It had puffy sleeves, just like a princess dress. They bought a tiara and a wand at the Halloween store to finish the costume. Kristina felt like a real princess in it.

I hope my dress still fits! she thought.

She opened up the closet door.

"BOO!"

Peter jumped out of the closet, making a scary face.

"Aaaaaaaah!" Kristina screamed.

Chapter Two

The Brave Princess

"Ha-ha!" Peter laughed, pointing at her. "I scared you!"

Kristina tried not to cry. "That's not funny, Peter!" she yelled.

Grandma Soo came into the room. "What is all this yelling about?"

"Peter jumped out of the closet and scared me!" Kristina said, pointing at her little brother. "And he didn't hang up his coat or backpack, either."

Peter made a face at her. "Tattletale!"

"Peter, say you are sorry for scaring your sister," Grandma Soo said.

Peter looked down at his shoes. "Sorry," he said softly.

"Good," said Grandma Soo. "Now go downstairs and pick up your things."

Peter left without arguing. Grandma Soo nodded at the closet.

"So, did you find your dress?" she asked.

Kristina looked at the closet. The door was open. But now she was afraid to go inside.

"What if something else is in there?" she asked quietly.

Grandma Soo sat down on the bed. She patted the spot next to her. Kristina sat down, too. Pixie crawled across the covers and climbed onto Kristina's lap. Kristina stroked the kitten's warm fur, and Pixie purred happily.

"Everyone is afraid of something, Kristina," Grandma Soo said. "But we are all brave inside. We just have to find that brave part within us."

"How do you do that?" Kristina asked.

Grandma Soo thought for a minute.

"I think you find it when you need it most," she said. "Remember the story I told you about the Princess and the Monster?"

Kristina nodded. "Can you tell it again?"

"It is a good story," said Grandma Soo. She cleared her throat and began to tell the story in her best storytelling voice.

"Long ago in Korea, there lived a young princess. She had fancy clothes and riches and everything else she could want. She was never afraid.

"Then one day, a terrible monster stormed into the palace and carried the princess away. The monster took her down deep, deep into the earth to his dark palace."

"Oh, no!" Kristina said.

"This monster was very, very ugly and very, very mean," her grandmother said. "He made the princess cook and clean for him all day and night.

"The princess wanted to escape the monster and go back home. She did not know how to escape, but she did not give up. Even though she was small, she was not afraid of the monster."

"Why wasn't she afraid?" Kristina asked, squeezing her eyes shut.

"Because anyone

can be brave, even a young princess," said Grandma Soo. "Do you want to know what she did?"

Kristina nodded.

"The princess made a sleeping potion from persimmon juice," her grandmother went on. "Then she made the monster's favorite stew and put the potion in it. The monster fell into a deep sleep."

"I know what happens next!" Kristina said.

"That's right," Grandma Soo said with a smile. "The princess climbed up, up, up until she saw the sunshine again."

"And they all lived happily ever after!" Kristina finished.

Grandma Soo smiled. "See? The princess was brave. She was not afraid of a big, mean monster." She pointed at the closet. "You are not afraid of a closet, are you?"

"No!" Kristina said, taking Pixie off of her lap. She jumped off of the bed, stood up tall, and walked to the closet.

But then she paused for a second. Maybe she was afraid of a closet after all.

What if there's a big ugly monster in there? she worried. But Grandma Soo said it was just a story. Besides, her closet was too small for a big monster. Kristina opened the door slowly.

There was no monster inside. Kristina found the orange princess dress and showed it to Grandma Soo.

"That might still fit you," Grandma Soo said, smiling kindly. "Why don't you try it on?"

Kristina tried on the dress. She looked in the mirror and smiled. A beautiful princess with shiny black hair and brown eyes stared back at her.

"It fits!" Kristina cried.

"Yes, it does," agreed Grandma Soo. "It is a very nice princess dress."

Kristina twirled around. "I can't wait until the ball!"

Chapter Three

The Best Dress?

The next day at school, everyone was talking about the ball. Kristina's teacher, Mrs. Underwood, had to keep telling them to be quiet during class!

Kristina waited and waited all morning. Finally, it was time for lunch. She could finally talk to her friends about the ball!

Kristina was so excited that she ran into the cafeteria when she was supposed to walk. She sat down at a table with all of her friends.

"Are you going to the Fall Ball?" Kristina asked them. "What are you going to wear?"

"I'm going to be an octopus!" said Chloe. She had curly red hair and freckles. "My costume's going to have eight arms!"

"Then you can eat eight cupcakes at once," joked Melissa. Everyone laughed.

"What are you going to be, Melissa?" Kristina asked.

"I'm going to be a mermaid," Melissa said, tossing her long blonde hair over one shoulder. She put a hand on top of her head. "My costume has a crown and everything."

"Mine does, too!" chimed in Ashley. She pulled a piece of paper from her lunch bag and slid it across the table. "I'm going to be a princess. My mom's getting me this costume."

The girls leaned in to look at the picture.

The dress was silver and pink. It had a wide skirt with lots of layers. The sleeves were puffy on top, and the arms were made of shiny material. There were silver flowers on the neck and around the waist.

"Ooh, it's beautiful," Kristina said. "If it was orange, it would be the best princess dress ever!"

"I'm so excited!" said Ashley.

All the girls began to talk, but Kristina was quiet. She was thinking about her orange princess dress.

It was a pretty dress. But Ashley's dress was much fancier! Suddenly, her orange dress felt very plain.

Kristina opened up her lunch bag. Grandma Soo had packed her a container of kimbap. They usually ate kimbap as a snack at home. Grandma Soo rolled up white rice and vegetables in a piece of dried seaweed. Then she cut the roll into slices.

Kristina liked peanut butter and jelly for lunch best, but kimbap was good, too. She popped a piece of it into her mouth and noticed Ashley was looking at her.

Suddenly, Kristina felt a little bit embarrassed. All of the other girls were eating sandwiches.

"Is that sushi?" Ashley asked.

"It's like sushi," Kristina said. "But it's kimbap. It's Korean."

"Cool," Ashley said. "I like sushi."

Ashley took a bite of her sandwich, and Kristina forgot about being embarrassed. The girls talked about the party as they ate their lunch.

"What are you going to be for the ball, Kristina?" Chloe asked.

"A princess," Kristina replied.

"Yay! We can be princesses together," Ashley said, taking a sip of her milk. "What does your dress look like?"

Kristina thought fast. "I'll draw it for you."

Kristina loved to draw, so her mom always packed a tiny tin of colored pencils and some paper with her lunch. Kristina took out the orange pencil — the shortest one in the tin, because she used it so much — and began to draw.

She drew a dress with a big skirt. Then she drew another skirt that looked like flower petals, on top of the big one. She added ruffles to the collar of the dress and pretty, puffy sleeves. Then she drew stars for buttons on the top of the dress.

"This is what my dress is going to look like," Kristina said,

holding up the paper to show the dress to her friends.

"It's soooo beautiful!" Ashley said, clapping her hands.

"I like the stars on it," said Chloe.

Melissa grinned at the girls around the table. "We'll all have the best costumes!"

Kristina looked down at her picture. It was a beautiful dress. There was only one problem.

Where was she going to get a dress like that?

Chapter Four

The Monster Mask

After school that day, Grandma Soo helped Kristina and Peter with their homework until Mr. and Mrs. Kim came home. Kristina's parents were both dentists who worked in the same office. That's why Grandma Soo lived with them. She watched Kristina and Peter while their parents worked.

Kristina gave her mom and dad a big hug when they got home. She wanted to ask them about getting a new princess dress right away, but she waited. Mrs. Kim was busy making dinner, and Mr. Kim was playing outside with Peter.

Kristina was very helpful for the rest of the night. She set the table without being asked. She dried the dishes after her father washed them.

When everything was clean, Kristina's parents sat at the kitchen table with Grandma Soo. They talked about the day as Grandma Soo sliced some bright orange persimmons. Kristina thought they looked like orange tomatoes, but they didn't taste like tomatoes at all. They were juicy and sweet. They were like the persimmons in the story Grandma Soo told her, except they didn't make you sleepy.

Kristina pulled the picture of the princess dress out of her backpack. She sat down next to her mom. Then she picked up a piece of persimmon and bit into it.

"Kristina, I hear you are very excited about the Fall Ball," said Mrs. Kim. "I think it will be fun, too. I signed us up to help with the decorations."

Just then, Peter ran into the room. *"Raaaaawr!"* He roared like a monster.

Peter had a mask over his head. The mask was furry and looked like a wolf with big, sharp teeth.

Kristina jumped in her seat. She almost screamed, but she thought of the brave

princess just in time. She kept her scream inside.

"Peter, what is that?" her mother asked.

Peter took off the mask. "It's my werewolf costume," he said. "It's for the Fall Ball."

Mrs. Kim looked at Mr. Kim. "Is that where you were at lunch today? Buying a mask for Peter?"

Mr. Kim smiled. "We wanted to surprise you."

"I don't like it," Mrs. Kim said with a frown. "It's very scary. He's only five!"

"It's not scary," said Peter. "Anyway, all the other kids are going as monsters, too."

Kristina hadn't thought of that. There might be lots of kids dressed as monsters at the Fall Ball. It wouldn't be easy to be a brave princess all the time.

"Kristina, are you going as a princess?" asked Mrs. Kim.

"Her dress from last Halloween still fits," Grandma Soo said. "She will look very pretty."

Kristina unfolded her drawing. "I think I want a new dress," she said. She showed the picture to her mom.

Mrs. Kim looked closely at it. "This is a very fancy dress," she said.

Pixie jumped up onto Kristina's lap. Grandma Soo laughed.

"Pixie wants to see the picture, too," she said.

"Maybe we can find one in a costume store," Kristina said. "Ashley is getting a fancy princess dress there. They might have an orange one, too."

"Let me see," said Grandma Soo. Mrs. Kim gave her the picture.

Grandma Soo nodded. "You want to

be an orange princess? I can sew you a beautiful orange dress."

"Really?" Kristina asked. Her eyes got wide.

"Grandma Soo can sew anything," said Mr. Kim.

Kristina ran around the table and hugged her grandmother. "Oh, thank you!"

At that moment, Mrs. Kim let out a little yell.

"A spider!" she cried, pointing. "Peter, get it!" A small black spider was crawling up the white kitchen wall.

Peter ran off into the living room. "No way!"

"I'll do it," said Kristina. She got a

paper cup from the bathroom. She put the cup over the spider, and it dropped inside. She carried the cup to the back door and let the spider out.

When she came back into the kitchen, Grandma Soo smiled at her.

"See, Kristina? That was very brave," she said.

"But I'm not afraid of spiders," Kristina said. That was true. Spiders and bugs never scared her. She looked at Peter's mask on the floor. "Only monsters."

"If you can be brave about spiders, you can be brave about anything," Grandma Soo told her.

Kristina hoped she was right. She had to be brave about monsters, or she wouldn't be able to go to the Fall Ball. And *that* would be terrible!

Chapter Five

A Fairy Godmother
and an Octopus

The next five days went by very, very slowly
while Grandma Soo worked on the orange
princess dress. She did all the sewing in her
bedroom, and did not let Kristina have
even one little peek.

Kristina tried to peek, anyway. She
tiptoed very quietly to Grandma Soo's
door. She looked through the keyhole, but
all she could see was her grandmother's

bed. Then she got down and looked through the crack in the bottom of the door.

"Not yet, Kristina," Grandma Soo called out. And Kristina ran away, her heart pounding. How did Grandma Soo know?

On Monday, Kristina went over to Chloe's house after school. Melissa came, too. Each girl brought her favorite princess doll.

"Let's pretend we're at a fancy ball," said Kristina. "We can practice for the real ball."

They all sat on the floor of Chloe's bedroom. Kristina looked around for things they could use.

"We need a carriage to take us to the ball," Kristina went on.

Chloe ran to her closet and came back with a shoe box. "How about this?"

"Perfect!" said Kristina. She put her princess doll in the shoe box, and her friends did the same.

Melissa frowned. "It doesn't look like a carriage."

"Of course not," Kristina said. "It's not done yet. Our fairy godmother has to come and turn it into a beautiful carriage for us."

"Ooh, I have a fairy!" Melissa cried. She reached into her pink backpack and took out a fairy doll.

"Perfect! That's our fairy godmother," said Kristina. "Now she has to do magic to turn the shoe box into a carriage."

Melissa waved the fairy around in the air. Then she talked in a funny high voice. "Abracadabra, turn this box into a carriage!"

"Poof!" added Kristina. "See? It's a beautiful orange carriage led by white horses."

"Can't it be a purple carriage?" Chloe asked, squinting at the shoe box.

"Or a pink one?" Melissa suggested.

"It's an orange *and* purple *and* pink carriage," Kristina said, her eyes sparkling. "And it's all glittery."

Melissa talked in the fairy voice again. "Get home by midnight, or the carriage will turn back into a shoe box," she warned.

Chloe's green eyes got wide. "Do you think we'll be able to stay up until midnight? My bedtime is nine on weekends."

Kristina was daydreaming. "Imagine if a *real* fairy godmother came to the ball? She could grant us wishes. She could turn our car into a beautiful carriage with horses."

"If it's a real ball, there might be a real fairy godmother," Melissa said hopefully.

Chloe's mom stepped into the room. "Chloe, can I borrow you for a second? I need you to try on your octopus costume."

"Sure, Mom," Chloe said, jumping up. She nodded to her friends. "Come see!"

They followed Chloe to the kitchen. The table was filled with bags of stuffing and purple material. Chloe's mom held up a hooded purple sweatshirt. It had six octopus arms dangling from it.

"I stuffed purple tights to make the arms," her mom said. "Try it on."

Chloe tried on the costume. She put the hood over her head.

"See? Six fake arms plus your two real arms makes eight," Chloe's mom said.

Chloe wiggled her real arms, and her

fake arms waved, too. "Hello, I'm an octopus!" she said. "Let's shake hands."

Kristina and Melissa giggled as they shook every one of Chloe's eight hands.

"It's a great costume," said Melissa. "We just got my mermaid costume from the store the other day. I can't wait to wear it!"

"My costume will be ready soon," Kristina said. "Yesterday, Grandma Soo said it was almost done."

"That reminds me, I told your grandmother I'd bring you home," said Chloe's mom. "Let's all take a walk."

Kristina felt a burst of excitement. Maybe her costume would be done when she got home!

Chapter Six

A Tiny Lie

When Kristina walked through the front door, she didn't see Grandma Soo. Then she heard her call from upstairs.

"Kristina, come here! I have something to show you."

Kristina was so excited that she tossed her orange backpack on the floor. She ran up the stairs.

"Is it done? Can I see it?" she asked, bursting into Grandma Soo's bedroom.

Grandma Soo stood in front of her

sewing machine with her hands behind her back. "I just finished," she said. With a big smile, Grandma Soo held the dress out in front of her.

At first, Kristina was confused.

The dress had a long orange skirt, but it wasn't big and puffy like the one Kristina had drawn. There wasn't a second skirt that looked like flower petals. Instead, there was a silk sash around the waist.

The top of the dress was white. There were no ruffles on the collar, and no star-shaped buttons. The sleeves were long and wide, instead of short and puffy. The collar and sleeves were edged with orange trim that had flowers on it.

Kristina wasn't sure what to say. "What is this?" she finally asked.

"It is your dress for the ball," said Grandma Soo. "Girls in Korea wear a dress like this when they need a very special outfit. It is orange, just like you wanted."

Kristina felt her face get warm. She thought Grandma Soo was going to sew the beautiful princess dress in her drawing. Instead, she made a boring old Korean dress! Kristina felt like crying, but she didn't want to hurt her grandmother's feelings.

"Thank you," Kristina said in a small voice. She gave Grandma Soo a hug. "It's very nice."

Kristina took the dress to her room. She closed the door behind her and flopped down on the bed. Her eyes filled with tears.

The dress was all wrong! It didn't look like the princess dress in her picture at all.

Too bad I don't have a real fairy godmother! Kristina thought.

She sat up and stared at the dress, trying to figure out what to do. She couldn't tell Grandma Soo she didn't like it. That would hurt her feelings.

But she didn't want to wear the dress, either.

"I wish there was no Fall Ball!" Kristina whispered, falling back on her bed.

There was a knock on the door, and her mom came into the room.

"Your father and I just got home," said Mrs. Kim. "Grandma Soo said she finished your dress. Is that it?"

Kristina sat up and nodded.

Mrs. Kim picked up the dress. "How pretty! It's just like the one she made for me when I was a little girl. But mine was green and red. I hope you thanked her."

"I did," Kristina said.

Her mom looked around the room. "We just need to find your tiara from last

year," she said. "Then you'll be a perfect princess."

No, I won't! Kristina wanted to say. *That is* not *a princess dress!*

But she couldn't say the words out loud. Grandma Soo had worked so hard. Her mother would think she was mean if she didn't like the dress. So Kristina thought of something else to say instead.

"I don't think I want to go to the Fall Ball," she told her mom.

Mrs. Kim looked puzzled. "Why not? It's all you've talked about for a week!"

"There will be scary costumes there," Kristina said. That part was true. She was worried about seeing the scary costumes. But that wasn't the real reason she didn't want to go to the ball. She didn't want to go because of the dress.

It wasn't really a lie, was it?

Maybe a tiny lie, Kristina thought. *Tiny lies aren't so bad.*

Her mom sat down on the bed next to her. "You shouldn't worry so much. There will be some scary costumes, and some funny ones, and some pretty ones, too. And the scary costumes are just that — costumes. Your dad and I will be there with you. It will be fun!"

"Do I have to go?" Kristina asked. "Can't I just stay home with Grandma Soo?"

Mrs. Kim shook her head. "I think it's important for you to go and see that the costumes aren't so scary," she said. "You'll have a good time, I promise. And you'll get to wear your beautiful new dress!" Mrs. Kim gave Kristina a hug. "I'm going to make dinner," she said, leaving the room.

Kristina looked down at the dress on her bed. It wasn't fair! Now she would have to look at scary costumes *and* wear the wrong dress to the ball.

But then Kristina got an idea. If she didn't have a costume, she couldn't go at all.

Kristina rolled up the dress into a ball. She opened up her closet and stuck the dress way in the back.

She would tell Grandma Soo that she lost the dress. Then she wouldn't have to go to the ball.

Kristina felt bad. Pretending to lose the dress was a big lie, not a tiny one.

What would a princess do? Kristina wondered.

A princess would ask her fairy godmother for help. But Kristina didn't have a fairy godmother.

She closed the closet door. She would tell the big lie.

It was better than hurting Grandma Soo's feelings . . . wasn't it?

Chapter Seven

Fun with Spiders

The next day at school, everyone was talking about the Fall Ball. It was only five days away! Kristina wished the Fall Ball would just go away. Every time she thought about the dress in the back of her closet, she got a bad feeling inside.

Ashley was very excited at lunch that day.

"We went to the costume store last night," she said. "I got my princess dress. It's perfect!"

"Mom finished my octopus costume last night," Chloe added.

Melissa looked at Kristina. "What about you? Did your grandma finish your dress?"

"Um, she's still working on it," Kristina said, looking down at her sandwich. "Anyway, I don't think I'm going to the ball."

"You're not?!" Chloe cried. "But you *have* to go."

"There will be too many scary costumes there," Kristina said quietly. "Lots of monsters. I really hate monsters."

"Me, too," said Melissa with a shiver.

Ashley shrugged. "They're not real. They're just costumes."

"But Peter tries to scare me all the time," Kristina said. "I bet he'll get all his little monster friends to scare me at the ball."

"Then just scare him back," Chloe suggested.

Kristina had never thought of that. "How?" she asked.

"I don't know," said Chloe. "Maybe you could wear a monster mask."

"He's not scared of monsters," Kristina replied.

Melissa scratched her head. "He must be scared of something."

Kristina frowned. "I don't know. But it's a good idea."

For the rest of lunch, while her friends talked about the Fall Ball, Kristina stayed very quiet. She was glad when school was over for the day. She didn't feel like hearing about the Fall Ball anymore!

After dinner that night, Mrs. Kim

announced that she was going to the party store.

"Come with me, Kristina," she said. "We need to get decorations for the Fall Ball."

Kristina didn't really want to go, but she agreed. And when they got to the store, she started to feel excited. There were so many decorations to choose from!

"We need some streamers," said Mrs. Kim.

"*Orange* streamers," Kristina told her.

Mrs. Kim smiled. "Of course. Orange is a very good color for a Fall Ball. We need to order some balloons, too."

"*Orange* balloons," said Kristina.

The store had all kinds of decorations. There were plastic pumpkins and chains of autumn leaves. There were scary decorations, too. Mrs. Kim picked up a bag of fake spiders.

"What about these?" she asked. "Do you think they're too scary?"

Kristina shook her head and grinned. "No. They're good."

"Of course," said Mrs. Kim. "I forgot how brave you were with that spider in the kitchen. Your little brother ran away!"

Kristina had forgotten that Peter ran away from the spider. Her smile got even wider.

"Definitely get the spiders, Mom," she said.

When they got home, Kristina took a handful of fake spiders from the bag. She went into Peter's room and put the spiders under his covers.

When it was time for Peter to get ready for bed, Kristina watched him go into his room. She tiptoed up to the door and peeked inside. Pixie followed her and looked inside Peter's room, like she knew something was about to happen.

Peter pulled down his covers. Then he jumped back. *"Aaaaaah!* Spiders!" he yelled.

He ran out of the room so fast that he almost knocked down Kristina! His eyes were wide. Kristina couldn't help giggling.

Mr. Kim came up the stairs. "Peter, what's wrong?" he asked.

"There are spiders in my bed!" Peter cried.

Mr. Kim went into Peter's room. He came back out holding the fake spiders in his hand. "Kristina, do you know how these fake spiders got into your brother's bed?" he asked.

"I put them there," Kristina said, looking down at her feet.

"No fair!" Peter said. "You scared me!"

"You scare me all the time!" Kristina shot back.

Mr. Kim sighed. "How about this? There's a new rule in this house: No more scaring each other. All right?"

"All right," Kristina and Peter both said, but Peter mumbled the words. He glared at Kristina.

Kristina just smiled. Now she knew why Peter liked to scare her all the time. Scaring people was fun!

Chapter Eight

Grandma Soo Finds Out

"So I put the fake spiders in his bed," Kristina told her friends before school the next day. "He yelled so loud!"

The girls all laughed.

"I bet he won't try to scare you now!" said Chloe. "Does this mean you're going to the Fall Ball after all?"

"I think so," Kristina said.

Her answer surprised her! But Kristina knew now that she really did want to go. The decorations were going to be so pretty. All of her friends would be there. There would be music and dancing and good things to eat, too.

Wearing the Korean dress wouldn't be *so* bad. At least it was orange! And Kristina knew she could still wear her princess crown and wand. She would take the dress out of the closet and find a way to smooth it out. Then Grandma Soo would never know she had crumpled it up into a ball.

Kristina felt happy for the first time in days. She skipped off of the school bus later that afternoon. Peter raced into the house ahead of her, as always. But Grandma Soo was not at the door. She always met them at the door!

Kristina headed inside, wondering what had happened. She didn't have to wonder long.

"Kristina? Come up here, please!" Grandma Soo called from upstairs.

Kristina walked up the steps. Grandma Soo was in Kristina's bedroom. Her hands were on her hips, and she was frowning.

"Kristina, I need you to try on your princess dress to make sure it fits," she said. "But I can't find it anywhere. Where did you put it?"

Kristina's mouth felt dry. She couldn't let Grandma Soo find out what she did to the dress!

"It's okay. I'll find it myself," Kristina said.

Grandma Soo shook her head. "I don't understand. A fancy dress like that should be in a safe place." She opened the closet door. "See? It's not hanging up."

Before Kristina could say anything else, Grandma Soo got down on her knees. "Maybe it fell off of the hanger," she said, looking around the bottom of Kristina's closet.

Kristina wished she could run out of the room. She heard Grandma Soo gasp.

"Here it is!"

Grandma Soo stood up and stepped out of the closet. She held the crumpled-up dress in her hands.

"This doesn't look like it fell off of the hanger," she said, frowning. "It looks like somebody crumpled it up on purpose."

Kristina peered down at her shoes. She didn't say anything. She just waited for Grandma Soo to yell at her.

But Grandma Soo didn't yell. Instead, she quietly left the room.

Kristina felt terrible. She had thought that a big lie would keep Grandma Soo's

feelings from getting hurt. But now
Grandma Soo was very hurt, and it was
all Kristina's fault!

What would a princess do? Kristina
took a deep breath.

She had to make things right.

Chapter Nine

A Real Fairy Godmother

A few minutes later, Kristina walked down the hall to Grandma Soo's room. The door was closed. Kristina knocked.

"Grandma Soo, may I please come in?" Kristina called.

"Yes," her grandmother answered in a soft voice.

Kristina gently pushed the door open. Grandma Soo sat in her chair with a sad look on her face. The crumpled-up dress was on her lap.

"I'm sorry, Grandma Soo," Kristina said. "I'm sorry I did that to the dress."

"I don't understand," Grandma Soo said. "This is a beautiful dress. When I was a little girl, I dreamed of having a dress like this. Why would you crumple it up like that?"

Kristina took a deep breath. She knew she had to tell the truth.

"It's a nice dress," she said. "But it's not a *princess* dress."

"Of course it is," Grandma Soo replied. "A princess would be proud to wear this dress."

Kristina was confused. "But Snow White and Cinderella don't wear dresses like that."

"It is a dress for a Korean princess," said Grandma Soo. "Like the princesses in the stories I tell you."

"But I don't *want* to be a Korean princess," Kristina blurted out. "I want to be a regular princess."

"That is silly," said Grandma Soo. "You are a Korean girl. A Korean girl should be a Korean princess."

"I'm also an American girl," Kristina told her. Then she looked down at her feet. Her parents had taught her not to talk back to grown-ups. Grandma Soo would be *really* angry with her now.

But Grandma Soo was quiet. Kristina glanced up and saw that her grandmother was thinking very hard.

"That is true," she said. "I forget that sometimes. You are a Korean girl and an American girl at the same time."

Grandma Soo walked to her sewing machine. She picked up the drawing of the dress Kristina had made. "This is the dress you wanted," she said. "It's very pretty. I just thought you would like the Korean dress better."

"The Korean dress is pretty, too," said

Kristina. "The orange skirt is beautiful."

Grandma Soo smiled. "I have an idea. Maybe we can make a dress for a princess who is Korean *and* American."

Kristina knew exactly what her grandmother meant. She jumped up. "Let me get my colored pencils," she said.

She came back a minute later and turned over her drawing. On the other side, she drew a new dress with her colored pencils. She started by drawing the Korean dress. Then she added some things from her first drawing.

Grandma Soo nodded. "That is very nice, and not too hard to do. We can finish it by Saturday."

"You mean I can help?" Kristina asked.

"Of course," Grandma Soo said. "It's about time I taught you how to sew."

Mrs. Kim took them to the fabric

store that night. For the rest of the week, Kristina helped Grandma Soo every day after school. Grandma Soo used shimmery material to make a flower petal skirt on top of the orange skirt. She put more flower petals around the collar.

Kristina cut stars out of silver material. Grandma Soo showed her how to sew them onto the dress by hand. Kristina sewed the stars onto the top of the dress. They looked so pretty!

Pixie was very interested in all of the sewing. She perched on Grandma Soo's dresser and watched them with her big blue eyes.

On Friday, the day before the dance, they finished the dress. Kristina tried it on and looked at herself in the mirror.

"It's beautiful!" she said. "It's just like a dress a fairy godmother would make."

Kristina saw Grandma Soo's smiling face in the mirror behind her. Then she gasped.

"It's you!" Kristina said.

Grandma Soo gave her a puzzled look.

"*You're* my fairy godmother," Kristina said, squeezing her in a big hug. "Just like in a fairy tale."

"That is silly," said Grandma Soo. But she had a very big smile on her face.

Kristina twirled around in her dress.

"The ball is tomorrow night! Can you turn our car into a coach with white horses?" Kristina asked.

"I don't think so," Grandma Soo replied. "I am the kind of fairy grandmother who makes dresses. I can't make horses."

Kristina twirled around again. She
didn't need a beautiful coach. She already
had a beautiful dress! "I can't wait until
tomorrow!"

Chapter Ten

The Best Ball of All

The next night, Kristina put on her perfect princess dress. She set a sparkly tiara on her head and picked up her princess wand. She slid her feet into her special princess shoes. They were flat shoes made of shiny silver material with orange and green and blue designs. Mrs. Kim had found them at the Asian market.

Kristina ran downstairs. Her mom wore a witch hat and a black dress. Mr. Kim was tying a vampire cape around his neck.

"Is it time to go yet?" Kristina asked.

"I just need to find my fangs," Mr. Kim replied.

Mrs. Kim gave Kristina a hug. "You look just like a beautiful princess!" she said.

"Thanks, Mom," Kristina said.

Peter ran into the room in his werewolf costume. He stomped right up to Kristina.

"Raaaaawr!" he roared.

"Peter, there is no more scaring in this house," Mrs. Kim said.

"That's okay, Mom," Kristina told her. "I know it's just pretend."

Mrs. Kim gave Kristina a surprised look. Then Mr. Kim held up some pointy plastic teeth. "Found them!"

Grandma Soo came into the living room carrying a silver tray.

"Here are some dumplings for the party," she said. "You can't have a party without dumplings."

"I wish you were going, Grandma," Kristina told her.

Grandma Soo waved her hand. "A party is no place for an old lady like me. You all go and have a good time. I'll see you when you get back."

Kristina climbed into the backseat of the car. After she put on her seat belt, she noticed something in the pocket of the seat in front of her.

It was a drawing of an orange pumpkin coach with four white horses. Kristina recognized Grandma Soo's handwriting on the picture.

This is the best I could do.
Have a good time at the ball!

"What's that?" Peter asked.

Kristina grinned. "It's a present from my fairy godmother."

Peter checked the pocket in front of him. "Did I get a fairy godmother present?"

"Only princesses have fairy godmothers. Werewolves don't," Kristina told him.

Peter folded his furry arms across his chest. Kristina looked at her little brother for a minute, then handed him the drawing.

"Here," she said. "We can share."

"Thanks," said Peter through his mask.

The drive to the school seemed to take forever! When they finally arrived, there were cars everywhere. Kids and their parents were walking into the school, and everyone wore a costume. There were lots of princesses, and even lots of monsters. But Kristina wasn't scared of any of them.

Kristina and her family walked through the crowd and entered the school gym.

Kristina stopped and stared. It looked beautiful! Yellow and orange lights shone on the walls. Orange balloons decorated the tables. She saw leaves and pumpkins and spiders everywhere she looked.

"I'm going to put the dumplings on the table," said Mrs. Kim.

There was a big open space in the gym where some kids were dancing. Kristina spotted Chloe in her octopus costume.

"I'm going to dance," Kristina told her dad. Then she ran to join her friends.

Chloe waved hello with all eight octopus arms. Melissa jumped out from behind her in her mermaid costume.

"Hi, Kristina!" Melissa cried. "You look nice. I love your dress!"

"Thanks," Kristina said, admiring Melissa's costume.

Ashley danced over to them in her princess dress.

"Wow," Kristina said. "You look beautiful!"

"Thanks," said Ashley. "But guess what? There are two other girls here with the exact same dress! I don't see anybody else with your dress on."

Kristina beamed proudly. "I helped my Grandma Soo make it."

The music got louder. Chloe waved her arms again. "Let's dance!"

Kristina danced and danced with her friends. When they got tired, they took a break. Everyone tried Grandma Soo's dumplings.

"These are so good!" Chloe said, with her mouth full.

"My mom never makes these," Melissa said.

"That's because they're Korean," Kristina told her.

Ashley slurped down a dumpling.

"Mmm. You're lucky to be Korean."

Kristina had never thought about it that way before. But Ashley was right! She was lucky. She got to eat yummy things like dumplings and persimmons. She got to hear the Korean stories Grandma Soo told her. And now she had a beautiful part-Korean princess dress.

"Yes, I am," Kristina replied.

Another song came on. "I love this song!" Melissa cried. "Let's dance!"

The girls danced until the regular lights went on in the gym. The ball was over so fast!

"Kristina, it's time to go!" Mrs. Kim called from across the gym.

Kristina hugged her friends good-bye and ran toward her family. After just a few steps, the silver shoe on her right foot slipped right off! Kristina ran back to get it.

Melissa's eyes were wide. "Kristina,

you lost your shoe at the ball. Just like Cinderella!"

Kristina stared at the shoe in her hand. "You're right," she said in awe. How magical!

"Kristina!" Peter yelled. "Mom wants you."

Chloe giggled. "Only Cinderella didn't have a little brother."

"And the handsome prince found her slipper," Ashley said.

Kristina put on her shoe and smiled. It didn't matter that she had a little brother, or that a handsome prince didn't find her shoe.

She had a dress, and a crown, and even a real live fairy godmother.

Kristina felt exactly like a real princess!

Make It Yourself!
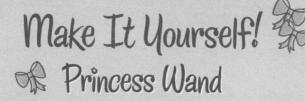 Princess Wand

Whip up a special sparkly wand to make *any* princess outfit more magical!

Level of difficulty: Medium
(You'll need some help from a grown-up.)

You Need:

- One wooden dowel rod, 12 inches long
- One foam ball, 1–3 inches in diameter
- Craft glue
- Acrylic paint
- Sequins
- Straight pins
- Ribbon

1. Put some glue on one end of the dowel rod. Then push the rod into the foam ball until it is about halfway into the ball.

2. Use a sponge brush to paint the surface of the ball. Let the paint dry.

3. Use pins to stick the sequins into the foam ball.

4. Tie the ribbon on the dowel rod underneath the ball. Now you're ready for any princess party!

Don't miss another royal
adventure— look for

Blue
Princess
Takes the
Stage

Turn the page for
a special sneak peek!

*"Oh, I am a magical princess!
And I live in a magical place . . ."*

"Emma Harrison! Are you singing again?" asked Mr. Parker.

A few kids laughed. Emma looked up from her math paper. She must have started singing while she was doing her subtraction problems.

"Sorry, Mr. Parker," Emma said. "I have an audition today."

"We're not doing *addition,* we're doing subtraction," Monica Sanchez said.

"I said 'audition,' not addition," Emma replied. "It's when you try out for a part in a play. We're doing *Princess Lyrica and the Choral Kingdom* at Miss Lisa's School of the Arts. I'm trying out for the part of Princess Lyrica."

Ever since Emma could remember, she dreamed of becoming an actress. And this was going to be her big chance!